CONT

# Eddie's News

Jody Martin and Ben Stubbs were walking home from school. Since they lived on the same block, they usually walked home together. They turned the corner onto Third Street.

"Eddie's?" Jody asked.

Ben nodded. He always wanted to go to Eddie's. He began skipping the last few steps.

Eddie's Bodega was a little grocery store
in their neighborhood in Quincy. It was
owned by Eddie Rivera. Jody, Ben, and
many of their friends went there almost
every day after school.

Jody and Ben liked buying a snack at
Eddie's. Most of all, they liked seeing Eddie.

Eddie knew all the children in the neighborhood. He was really nice. Sometimes Eddie gave the children an extra treat, "on the house." Sometimes he told them stories about the old days. He even knew Jody's parents when they were little!

Ben and Jody opened the door and walked into the store.

"Hi, Eddie!" they said. "What's up?"

"Buenas tardes, muchachos," said Eddie. "Actually, something *is* up. Do you know what next month is?"

The children shook their heads.

"Next month is the thirtieth anniversary of Eddie's Bodega!" said Eddie.

"Cool!" said Ben.

"I'm going to make a banner for the front of the store," said Eddie. "Do you want to come by in a few days and help me with it?"

"Sure, Eddie!" said Jody. "We'll help!"

Ben and Jody each picked out a snack.
They took out money to pay.

"That's all right, muchachos," said Eddie.
"It's on the house!"

# Ben's Idea

Ben and Jody walked to Ben's home. They were sitting on the front steps when Tina Perez and Brad Ming came by.

"Guess what?" Ben said. "Next month is Eddie's anniversary."

"I thought Eddie wasn't married," said Tina.

"Not that kind of anniversary," said Jody. "It's the  anniversary of Eddie's Bodega. It's been open thirty years."

"Wow!" said Brad. "That's a long time!"

Ben told Tina and Brad about the banner Eddie was making. "You should come and help, too," he said to Tina and Brad.

Then he said, "I wish we could do something for Eddie's anniversary."

"Yeah," said Jody. "Eddie's always doing things for everyone else."

"That's right!" said Brad. "He donates food from his store to help poor people."

"He finds homes for stray cats and dogs," said Tina.

"And he gives us free snacks!" added Ben, laughing.

"But what could we do?" asked Tina.

"I know!" said Ben, raising his hands. "We could give Eddie a party! An anniversary party!"

Jody put one hand on her chin as she always did when she was thinking. Then she smiled. "That's a great idea!" she said.

"I'll bet my mom and dad will help," Jody added.

"Mine, too," said Tina.

"My parents will want to be a part of this," Brad joined in.

Ben turned to go inside. "Why don't you guys come in? We've got a lot of work to do!"

# ⚡ Chapter 3 ⚡
# Making Plans

Jody, Tina, and Brad sat down at the kitchen table. Ben got Jody a piece of paper and a pencil. At the top of the paper, she carefully wrote *Things we need*.

"OK," said Jody. "What do we need for a party?"

"I know!" said Ben. "Food!"

Jody wrote down *Food*. Then she asked, "Where are we going to have the party?"

"Better write that down, too," said Tina. She didn't want to forget anything.

Ben, Jody, Brad, and Tina thought of more things. Jody wrote everything down. When they were finished, the list looked like this.

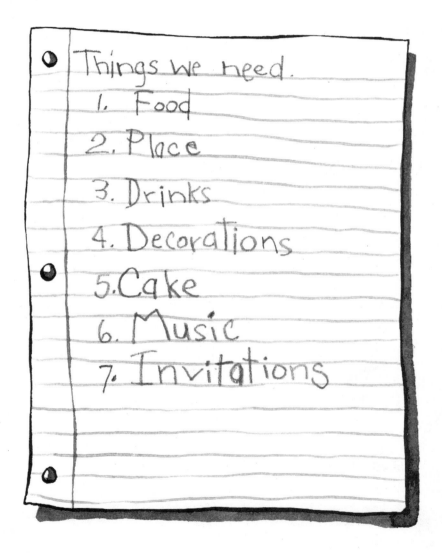

Things we need.
1. Food
2. Place
3. Drinks
4. Decorations
5. Cake
6. Music
7. Invitations

Ben's dad came into the kitchen. "What are you kids working on?" he asked.

"Dad!" Ben shouted. "Look at this!"

"Hi, Mr. Stubbs," said the kids.

Everyone began talking at once. They were trying to tell Ben's dad about Eddie's anniversary.

"Slow down! Slow down!" said Mr. Stubbs, laughing. "This sounds very exciting. But if everyone speaks at the same time, I can't understand what you're saying."

Ben grabbed the list and showed it to his father. They took turns telling him about Eddie's anniversary and their idea for a party.

"A party's a great idea!" said Mr. Stubbs. "I bet the whole neighborhood will want to come."

Mr. Stubbs sat down at the table with Ben, Jody, Brad, and Tina. He looked over the list. He said he would make a cake with a picture of Eddie's Bodega on it. Ben put a check next to the word *Cake*. His dad told the group not to forget plates, cups, napkins, forks, knives, and spoons. Jody added them to the list.

"What else do we need?" asked Tina.

"Let's see," said Mr. Stubbs.

# Chapter 4

# Everyone Pitches In

Soon after, Jody, Tina, and Brad went home. They all wanted to tell their families about the plans for Eddie's anniversary.

At dinnertime that night, Jody told her mom and dad about the party. "That's right," said Mr. Martin. "Eddie's been around since I was just a little boy. I'm 34 now, so it must be thirty years."

"Who can we invite to the party?" Jody asked. "I want to ask people who know Eddie. I don't want to forget anyone."

Mr. Martin got pencil and paper and began writing. Then he gave Jody a list. It had names, addresses, and phone numbers on it.

"Here, Jody," he said. "You can use this list. It has all the neighbors on it. Invite everyone!"

Just then the phone rang. It was Brad.
"Guess what?" said Jody when she hung up. "Brad told his dad about the party. Mr. Ming said we can have it in the place where he and Eddie go to singing practice for the community chorus. Wait until I tell Ben and Tina."

Jody rushed back to the telephone to call Ben first.

"That's great!" said Ben when he heard the news. "Mark that on the list."

Jody got the list. She put a check next to the word *Place*.

The next day, Ben and Jody didn't stop at Eddie's on their way home from school. They went straight home to Ben's house and sat on the steps. Brad and Tina soon joined them. A few more children stopped by.

"What's this about a party?" asked Ricky García.

Ben and Jody told him what was up.

Tina showed Ricky the list.

"Music?" said Ricky. "No problem. I know I can get my uncle Juan to play. He'd do anything for Eddie."

Ricky's uncle was a famous musician. He was in a band that played music all over the country.

"That's great!" said Tina. She put a check next to the word *Music*.

"Now we have to do something about invitations," Jody said.

"I can do one on my computer!" Brad jumped up.

That night, Brad's dad helped him make invitations on the computer. On the front they wrote these words.

COME ONE, COME ALL!
COME CELEBRATE!
WITH A FRIEND AND
NEIGHBOR
WHO'S REALLY GREAT!
IT'S THE 30TH ANNIVERSARY
OF EDDIE'S STORE!
LET'S ALL WISH HIM
THIRTY MORE!

The inside looked like this.

IT'S A SURPRISE PARTY!
FOR Eddie Rivera
Eddie's Bodega — 30th Anniversary
DATE: Saturday, October 16
TIME: 6:00 P.M.
PLACE: Quincy Hall
R.S.V.P.: Ben Stubbs 555-1214
or
Jody Martin 555-6798
Please call and tell us what you can bring.

The next day, Brad showed Ben, Jody, and Tina the invitations. Everyone helped write addresses on the envelopes and get them mailed. They couldn't wait until October 16.

# Chapter 5
## Keeping the Secret

Two days later, Ben, Jody, Brad, and Tina went to Eddie's after school. Eddie had a big piece of cloth.

"Hey!" he said. "I haven't seen you kids in a few days. Want to help me paint in the letters on my banner?"

"Sure," they said.

Eddie handed them aprons. He gave them paintbrushes. Then they got to work. Brad made big brush strokes, trying to fill in the letters. Jody worked more slowly, making sure her paint did not go outside the letter outlines.

"This will look great when I put it up in front of the store," said Eddie.

The children giggled. They were thinking about the party next month and trying not to say anything.

"What's so funny?" Eddie asked.

"Oh, nothing," said Jody. "Just a joke we heard."

"I would love to hear a joke," Eddie said. He grinned at the painters.

"I can't remember it all," Jody said quickly. "I'm not a good joke teller anyway."

"OK," Eddie said. He looked a little puzzled.

Ben looked around the store. He wanted to change the subject. A picture on the counter caught his eye.

"Who is that?" Ben asked.

Eddie turned to look. "That's my nephew, Carlos Ruiz," said Eddie. "He lives in Puerto Rico with my sister, Anna. Anna and her husband have three children. The older ones are 18 and 21. Carlos is the baby. Only he's not a baby anymore. He's already 10."

"Same age as we are!" said Jody.

"That's right," said Eddie. "I can hardly believe it. The last time I saw Carlos, he was only two. He must be a big boy by now. Anna and I write letters and call, but we don't get to visit very often. I really miss them."

"That's too bad," Tina said.

"Does he like baseball?" Brad asked.

"Oh, sure!" Eddie replied. "We often talk about baseball on the phone. If they could visit, I would like to take Carlos to a game here."

Eddie looked at the picture thoughtfully. Then he sighed. "Someday soon I would like to go to Puerto Rico to see Anna and her children."

Eddie went back to work on the banner. The children helped for a while, but it was hard to concentrate. They kept thinking about the party. Ben almost said something, but caught himself just in time. It was hard to keep their secret from Eddie!

# 🌟 Chapter 6 🌟
# Getting It All Together

A few days later, Ben and Brad were going over the plans for the party. Brad was spending the night at Ben's.

Brad's dad, Mr. Ming, was going to bring Eddie to the party. He was going to say there was an extra singing practice that night. Eddie wouldn't suspect a thing.

Tina's mom would get the decorations and the paper supplies, such as paper plates, cups, napkins, and tablecloths. Almost everyone had called and said they were coming. Lots of people were bringing food and drinks. Everything was set.

But Ben wasn't smiling.

"What's the matter?" asked Brad.

"I don't know," said Ben. "It seems as if we're forgetting something."

Ben paced around the room. Then he tossed his basketball through the hoop a couple of times.

"We went over Jody's list a hundred times!" said Brad. "What could we have forgotten?"

Suddenly, Ben stopped. "I know!" said Ben. "A present! We need to get Eddie a present!"

"But what?" asked Brad. "Eddie has everything he needs. He always says so."

"I don't know," said Ben, but he was thinking hard.

Later, Ben was still thinking about a present for Eddie when his father came into the room.

"What's wrong, Ben?" asked his dad.

"We don't have a present for Eddie," Ben said.

"The party is more than enough," said his dad.

"I know," said Ben. "But I still wish we could get Eddie something special."

"What do you think we can do?" the boys wondered.

## ~ Chapter 7 ~
# The Present

A couple of days later, Ben and Jody stopped at Eddie's. The party was only two weeks away.

"Look, guys!" Eddie said. "Doesn't it look great?"

Eddie had put the banner up. It really did look great.

"We'll have to get Tina and Brad over here to see it," Jody said.

Jody and Ben followed Eddie inside the store.

"And look at this," Eddie said. He showed them a picture of the store with the banner. "I'm sending it to my sister, Anna. It's too bad she can't see it in person."

Ben looked at the picture. Then he looked at Eddie. He could see how much Eddie missed Anna. Suddenly, he had an idea.

"That's it!" Ben whispered to Jody.
"That's what?" Jody asked.

Ben wouldn't say. Instead, he quickly picked out a snack and paid for it. He told Eddie they had a lot of homework to do. He almost pushed Jody toward the door. Jody glanced at Eddie. She saw he was wondering what Ben was up to.

"Come on, Jody! See you later, Eddie!" Ben called as they left.

"What's up?" Jody asked when they got outside.

"I was thinking that the only thing we forgot to plan was a really great present for Eddie," Ben said.

"That's a good idea, Ben," Jody agreed, "but what could we get for him that would be really great?"

"Brad and I have been wondering the same thing," Ben replied. "When we were in the store just now, I thought of the perfect present."

"What?" asked Jody.

"We have to get Eddie's sister, Anna, and his nephew Carlos to come to the party," Ben replied.

"But that's impossible," said Jody. "They live all the way in Puerto Rico."

Ben stopped and thought. "I guess you're right," he said. "But it's a good idea, isn't it?"

"Sure, Ben," said Jody. "It's a great idea."

That night, Ben was reading the newspaper with his dad. He was turning the pages to get to the sports section. Just then he saw a big ad with an airplane on it.

"Hey!" Ben shouted. "Look at this! For $199, we can get two round-trip tickets. We can buy the tickets for Eddie's sister and his nephew to come to the party."

"What's all this about?" asked Ben's dad.

Ben told his father about Eddie's sister, how much Eddie missed her, and the nephew he hadn't seen for so many years. Then he told his dad about his idea of getting Anna and Carlos to Eddie's party.

"What do you think, Dad?" asked Ben as he pointed to the newspaper ad.

"Well, son," said his dad, "let's see. How many families are coming to the party?"

Ben got his list of the names of people who had called him. He also got the list of people who had called Jody. He counted the people who had said yes.

"Twenty," he said.

"What if everyone put in a little money?" his dad suggested.

Ben knew what his dad was getting at. He figured it out in his head. "If the tickets are $200, and there are 20 families, we would need $10 from each family."

"Exactly," said his dad.

"I bet we could do that," said Ben.

"Wait a minute," said his dad. "First, you have to find out if Anna and her son will come."

"How can we do that?" said Ben. "We don't have her telephone number or her address. And we can't ask Eddie for it. That would give away the surprise."

Ben and his dad tried to think of a way.

"There must be SOME way to get that number," Ben said as he tapped his fingers on the table.

"Well, stop worrying about it now," his dad said. "Dinner is ready."

## Chapter 8
# The Plan Works

The next day, Ben and Jody stopped at Eddie's on their way home from school. Brad and Tina were with them. Ben had told them about his idea for buying the plane tickets. Together they had come up with a plan.

"Hi!" said Eddie. "I'm really busy. I don't know what's up, but I'm getting big orders this week. Victor Gonzalez just ordered 6 cases of soda. Kim Hito ordered 12 bags of pretzels. Think you can help me get them from the back, muchachos?"

"Sure," Ben said. Then Ben gave Tina a signal.

While Ben, Brad, and Jody were in the stockroom with Eddie, Tina went behind the counter. She knew Eddie kept a list of numbers by the phone. Sure enough, Anna's number was there. As quick as she could, Tina copied the number on a sheet of paper.

Later that afternoon, Tina's mother called Eddie's sister while Brad, Tina, Jody, and Ben tried to be quiet. Mrs. Perez introduced herself in Spanish and told Anna about the party. As she told Anna about the plan for Eddie's 30th anniversary celebration, she switched to English.

"I know it sounds crazy," said Mrs. Perez, "but the children love Eddie. They want to do something really special for him. This will be the community's gift. If we get the tickets, will you come?"

Tina couldn't wait to find out what Anna said. "Well?" she asked after her mom hung up. The others crowded close.

"Anna said yes!" answered Mrs. Perez.

All four children jumped up and down at the same time. Their plan was really going to work. They could hardly wait to see Eddie's face when he saw Anna and Carlos at the party. This was going to be a real celebration!

The children didn't have much time. They spent the next few days collecting money from the families. They also worked hard to put in some money of their own.

Ben cashed in his penny collection and got $8. Jody and Tina collected bottles and made $5 each. Brad delivered newspapers. They gave their parents the money to put toward the gift.

By the end of the week, they had done it. They had collected $200. On Saturday, Mr. Stubbs went to the travel agent to buy the tickets. He and the agent worked it out so that Anna could pick up the tickets at the airport in Puerto Rico.

When Ben and his dad got home, Mr. Stubbs called Anna to tell her about the plans.

"We'll see you on Saturday, October 16," said Anna Ruiz. "It will be great to see Eddie again. Carlos is so excited he can't sit still."

"We're all looking forward to meeting you. Goodbye," said Mr. Stubbs.

"Adios," said Anna.

# ᘒ Chapter 9 ᘖ
## Saturday at Last

Saturday, October 16, took forever to come. Finally the day arrived. Ben woke up early. He bounded out of bed. He couldn't wait. He was going with Tina and her mom to pick up Anna Ruiz and her son, Carlos, at the airport.

Ben's dad was up early, too. He wanted to get to his bakery as soon as possible. It would take him all morning to make the cake for the party.

When they got to the airport, Ben, Tina, and Mrs. Perez went to the gate. Through the window they watched the plane land. Then, in just a few minutes, people began coming down the walkway from the plane. Tina spotted a woman with a boy.

"Carlos!" yelled Tina.

"Yes!" said the boy. Carlos and his mom came over and introduced themselves.

"Hello! I'm Anna Ruiz and this is my son, Carlos. It's wonderful to meet you," she said.

"I recognized you from your picture," Tina said.

As they walked to where they could pick up the suitcases, Mrs. Ruiz and Mrs. Perez chatted in Spanish. The children quickly told Carlos about the party.

Mrs. Perez took Mrs. Ruiz and Carlos to
Jody's house, where they spent the rest of
the day. They wanted to be sure Eddie
didn't see them until the party. Ben and
Jody played a video game with Carlos.
Slowly the time went by.

## 👒 Chapter 10 🔮
# Surprise!

At 5 o'clock they all went over to Quincy Hall. Tina and Brad were already there with their families. They had set up all the tables and chairs. They had decorated the hall with balloons. They had even put up a banner. Everything looked great. Ricky García was already there, too. He was helping his uncle and the band set up their instruments on the little stage.

"My, my!" exclaimed Mrs. Ruiz. "You did all this for Eddie? Now I know why he won't leave Quincy and come back to Puerto Rico. He has such wonderful friends and neighbors here, it's no wonder he doesn't want to leave."

Other people began arriving with food and drinks. Mr. Stubbs and Mr. Martin brought in the cake and put it on a table. Jody and Ben introduced Mrs. Ruiz and Carlos.

Soon it was 6:15. Eddie would be coming with Mr. Ming in fifteen minutes. Mrs. Ruiz and Carlos went to wait in another room.

When Eddie came in with Mr. Ming, everyone yelled, "SURPRISE!"

Wow, was he surprised! He just stood frozen in one spot for a few seconds. Then he looked around. A big smile broke out on his face. He couldn't believe everyone had planned a party for him.

"Wait!" called Jody, Tina, Brad, and Ben. "Eddie, we've got a bigger surprise for you."

Jody and Ben left the room. Everyone became very quiet. Eddie couldn't imagine what the children were going to bring out for him.

Then he saw them come back with Anna and Carlos. He was so surprised he almost didn't recognize them at first.

Then Eddie cried, "Anna! Carlos! But how did you get here? How did you know?" He was stumbling over his words.